A Timeless Christmas Romance

A Nostalgic Holiday Love Story of Second Chances and Time Travel

Evangeline Winters

Copyright © 2024 by Evangeline Winters

All rights reserved.

No part of this book may be reproduced in any form or by any electronic or mechanical means, including information storage and retrieval systems, without written permission from the author, except for the use of brief quotations in a book review.

Contents

Prologue	1
1. Disillusioned Christmas	5
2. The First Journey – Wartime Christmas (1940s)	11
3. Breaking Traditions – Disco Christmas (1970s)	17
4. Unveiling the Past – Jack's Secret (1920s)	28
5. Falling in Love Through Time	39
6. The Final Choice – Christmas Eve	45
7. A Timeless Christmas Love	50
8. Afterword by Evangeline Winters	59

Prologue

The soft chime of a clock echoed in the quiet of the night, its ticking a reminder that time was always moving, always slipping through the cracks of reality. Outside, the streets of New York City lay blanketed in a fresh layer of snow, the world hushed in anticipation of Christmas morning. But in the dim light of an old, forgotten shop on a side street no one seemed to notice, time worked differently.

INSIDE, Jack stood behind the counter of his antique store, the familiar weight of the pocket watch resting in his palm. The watch, delicate yet powerful, shimmered faintly in the soft light, its intricate engravings worn smooth from decades of use. He had held this watch for what felt like an eternity, each tick a reminder of the countless Christmases he had witnessed, each year a new reflection of love, loss, and hope.

. . .

For Jack, Christmas had always been bittersweet. He had seen it in its many forms—glamorous, simple, joyful, and painful—each era carrying its own magic. But every year, as the lights flickered and the snow fell, the ache of the past lingered like a shadow, a reminder of the love he had once lost.

The world outside his shop had moved on. Years, decades, and even centuries had passed, but Jack remained. The keeper of time. The one who watched, but never fully belonged.

Until now.

A soft knock on the door startled him from his thoughts, and Jack looked up, his gaze flickering to the frosted glass. It was late—too late for customers. He had long since stopped expecting anyone to wander into the shop at this hour, especially on Christmas Eve. But something in the air felt different tonight, a subtle shift he couldn't quite explain.

He placed the watch back on the counter, his fingers lingering over its familiar surface, before moving toward the door. As he opened it, the cold air rushed in, carrying with it the crisp scent of winter and the promise of something new.

And there, standing in the glow of the streetlight, was a woman. She looked lost, her eyes filled with the kind of weariness Jack knew all too well.

"Can I help you?" he asked, his voice soft, though he already knew the answer.

. . .

THE WOMAN HESITATED FOR A MOMENT, glancing behind her as if uncertain how she had ended up here. Then she met his gaze, something shifting in her expression—something Jack recognized from all the Christmases he had seen before.

"I DON'T KNOW," she said quietly, stepping inside. "But I think I'm supposed to be here."

JACK'S HEART tightened as he closed the door behind her, the watch on the counter gleaming in the soft light, its tick-tock filling the room like a heartbeat.

TIME, it seemed, was about to shift once again.

AND FOR THE first time in a long while, Jack wondered if this Christmas might hold more than memories.

Disillusioned Christmas

Snowflakes spiralled lazily through the crisp evening air, blanketing the streets of New York City in a serene, white stillness that sharply contrasted with the hustle of holiday shoppers and twinkling lights lining every window. The city was alive with Christmas spirit, but Emma Turner barely noticed. Her breath clouded the air as she walked aimlessly down the street, her feet leading her nowhere in particular. She tugged her scarf tighter around her neck, trying to shield herself from the cold, though it wasn't just the chill of winter she felt—it was the coldness inside her.

CHRISTMAS USED to mean something to her. She used to revel in it: the magic, the warmth, the traditions, the sense of belonging. But now, at thirty-four, standing on the other side of a painful breakup, it all felt like a hollow spectacle. Her heartache had sucked the joy out of the season. She knew her family would be expecting her at the big annual Christmas gathering, but she couldn't bear the thought of sitting through the same tired rituals, forced smiles, and the ever-present question: *So, when are you going to settle down?*

SETTLING DOWN. Love. It all felt like a cruel joke now.

HER PHONE BUZZED in her coat pocket, but she didn't pull it out. It was probably her mom checking in, or maybe her sister, eager to talk about her engagement. Emma kept walking, pushing through the throngs of people, avoiding the bright, festive shop windows that reminded her of everything she no longer had—a partner to share the holiday with, the kind of love that made Christmas special.

She turned down a side street, hoping to escape the crowds. The alley was dimly lit, a stark contrast to the bustling main street, and it seemed quieter here, like she'd stepped into another world. The snow muffled the sounds of the city, and for a moment, she could almost believe she was the only person left in New York. She glanced around, noticing a row of darkened storefronts—old, forgotten shops with dusty windows and faded signs. Then, something caught her eye.

AT THE VERY end of the alley stood a small, unassuming shop she'd never noticed before. It looked like it belonged to another time, with its quaint, wooden door and a faded sign that read "Timeless Treasures." The display window was dim, yet something about it pulled her closer. Without really thinking, Emma stepped toward the door, brushing the snow from her coat before reaching for the handle.

. . .

THE BELL above the door jingled softly as she entered, and the warmth of the shop enveloped her immediately. The scent of wood polish and something faintly spicy—cloves, perhaps—filled the air. The space was small, cluttered with shelves that seemed to bend under the weight of the strange, old objects they held. Odd trinkets, vintage ornaments, and worn-out books lined the walls, and a soft, golden glow from an antique lamp bathed everything in a warm, amber light.

"CAN I HELP YOU WITH SOMETHING?"

EMMA JUMPED at the sound of the voice. She hadn't noticed anyone else in the shop, but now, standing behind the counter, was a man she hadn't seen when she walked in. He was tall, with dark, tousled hair and a hint of stubble on his jaw. His eyes, however, were what struck her most—deep and warm, yet carrying a weight of time behind them, as if they held secrets long forgotten. He smiled, but there was something knowing in that smile, something that set her on edge.

"Sorry," Emma stammered. "I didn't mean to intrude. I was just... curious."

"You're not intruding," the man said, stepping around the counter. "I'm Jack. And I don't believe in coincidences, especially when it comes to this shop." He gestured around the room with a sweeping hand. "It tends to draw people in when they need it."

Emma furrowed her brow. "When they need it?"

JACK NODDED, his expression shifting to something more serious. "People come here when they're searching for something. Maybe you don't know what you're looking for yet, but you'll find it here. Or, perhaps, it'll find you."

Emma tried to smile, but the weight of his words made her uneasy. She wasn't searching for anything—except maybe a way to escape the melancholy that had been hanging over her for months. She stepped closer to one of the shelves, running her fingers over a collection of old pocket watches, each one slightly different but all bearing the marks of time.

"These are beautiful," she murmured.

"Ah, yes," Jack said, coming to stand beside her. He picked up one of the watches, a small, ornate piece with intricate engravings on its case. "This one is particularly special." He held it out to her. "Go on, take a closer look."

Emma hesitated, then took the watch from his hand. It felt heavier than it looked, and as she turned it over in her palm, she noticed a strange inscription on the back. The words were small, almost too faded to read, but there was something familiar about them, something that tugged at a distant memory she couldn't quite place.

"What does it say?" she asked.

Jack's smile returned, a little softer now. "It says, 'Time is the only thing we can't get back, but sometimes, just sometimes, it lets us visit.'"

Emma's heart skipped a beat, and she looked up at him, confused. "What does that mean?"

Jack met her gaze, and for a moment, the weight of the world seemed to hang between them. "It means this isn't just any watch, Emma." He paused, letting the words sink in. "This watch can take you to Christmases of the past. To times and places you thought were lost forever."

A chill ran down her spine, and not because of the cold.

"That's impossible."

Jack's smile deepened, and there was a glint of something almost mischievous in his eyes. "Is it?"

Emma opened her mouth to argue, but something in the air shifted. The room seemed to grow smaller, or perhaps it was the walls closing in. The glow of the lamp softened, and the world outside the shop faded from her mind. She felt an odd pull, a quiet hum deep inside her chest. A memory surfaced—a Christmas long ago, one filled with laughter, warmth, and the unmistakable sense of magic that had once surrounded the holiday. A time before her heart had been broken. Before everything had changed.

"Would you like to find out?" Jack's voice broke through the haze of her thoughts.

Emma swallowed hard, her fingers tightening around the pocket watch. She should leave. She should toss the watch back onto the shelf and walk out of the shop. But something stopped her. Maybe it was the way Jack looked at her, or maybe it was the unbearable weight of the sadness she'd been carrying for so long. A tiny spark of hope flared within her, fragile but bright.

"I—" Emma began, but the words died in her throat. Instead, she nodded, unable to trust her voice.

Jack's smile softened. "Then hold on tight, Emma. Christmas is about to take on a whole new meaning."

Before she could question what was happening, the world around her began to shimmer and blur, as though the very air had been stirred by an unseen force. The warmth of the shop vanished, replaced by a sudden rush of cold. The floor seemed to fall away beneath her, and for a moment, she felt weightless, as though she were suspended in time itself.

And then, as quickly as it had started, the sensation ended. The world snapped back into focus, and Emma found herself standing in the middle of a bustling, snow-covered street. But this was no longer the New York she knew.

SOMEHOW, *impossibly, she had been transported to a different time —a different Christmas.*

THE ADVENTURE HAD BEGUN.

The First Journey – Wartime Christmas (1940s)

The cold air hit Emma's face like a slap, pulling her back into the present—or was it the past? She blinked rapidly, trying to make sense of what had just happened. The bustling streets of modern New York were gone, replaced by a small, sleepy town blanketed in snow. She stood at the edge of a cobblestone road, staring in disbelief as men and women, dressed in clothing from another era, hurried by with armfuls of brown paper-wrapped parcels and baskets. The storefronts were lined with simple, hand-painted signs, and the soft glow of gas lamps illuminated the foggy evening.

THIS CAN'T BE REAL. And yet, the snow beneath her boots felt real, the smell of coal smoke in the air was unmistakable, and the sound of a train's whistle in the distance pulled her attention to the small station down the road.

Emma clutched the pocket watch in her hand, her heart racing. Jack had said this would happen, that this watch could take her to Christmases long past. But she hadn't truly believed it—how could she? Yet here she was, standing in a world that seemed to belong to the 1940s, to a time she had only ever read about in history books.

Jack had transported her to another era.

Emma wrapped her arms around herself, suddenly aware of how out of place she looked in her modern wool coat and scarf. The people around her were bundled in heavy, worn-out jackets, most of them fraying at the edges, their shoes scuffed from use. Their faces were marked by a quiet weariness, as though the weight of the world hung on their shoulders. The war, she realized. This was the middle of World War II.

She could feel it in the air—the uncertainty, the tension. And yet, beneath it all, there was something else, too. Something hopeful. A sense of resilience, as if the spirit of Christmas was still fighting to survive despite the hardships.

Curiosity tugged at her, and Emma found herself walking toward the train station. She wasn't sure what she was looking for, but she felt a strange pull, as though this place had something to show her. As she approached, she noticed the station was crowded with people. Families clustered together, mothers holding tightly to small children, elderly couples huddled close, their breath visible in the frigid air. And then, there were the soldiers—young men in uniform, some standing tall and proud, others with eyes full of uncertainty and fear.

. . .

THE TRAIN SAT on the tracks, its engine hissing with steam, ready to depart. Emma watched as one soldier bent down to embrace a young woman, her hands gripping the front of his coat as though she were trying to memorize the feel of him, to hold on to this moment for as long as possible. Tears streaked her face, but she was smiling, whispering something to him that Emma couldn't hear over the murmur of the crowd. The soldier smiled back, though his own eyes glistened with unshed tears. He kissed her forehead gently, and then, with a final squeeze of her hand, he turned and boarded the train.

Emma's chest tightened as she watched the scene unfold, feeling like an intruder on something too intimate, too raw. She turned away, giving the couple their privacy, though the image of their goodbye stayed with her. This was Christmas in wartime—a time when families were torn apart, when love was tested by the uncertainties of the world.

A SUDDEN GUST of wind sent snow swirling around her, and she pulled her scarf tighter, trying to ward off the chill. As she did, a small group near the entrance of the station caught her eye. A family—two parents and their teenage daughter—stood together in silence. The father, wearing an old overcoat and a wool hat pulled low over his ears, held a small, wrapped package in his hands. The daughter, no more than sixteen, clung to her mother's arm, her face pale and drawn.

The mother was speaking quietly, her voice barely audible above the wind. "We'll be alright," she said, though her voice trembled. "We'll have a simple Christmas this year, but we'll make do, won't we, Lizzie?"

The daughter nodded, though her eyes were fixed on the ground.

Emma's heart ached at the sight. This family, like so many others, was trying to hold onto something—hope, love, faith in the future—while the war raged on. She wondered how many people had spent their Christmases this way, clinging to traditions in the face of unimaginable loss.

Suddenly, she felt a presence beside her. She turned, startled, to find Jack standing there, his hands tucked into the pockets of his long coat, his expression solemn as he watched the scene unfold.

"Why did you bring me here?" Emma asked, her voice quiet.

"To show you that even in the hardest of times, Christmas has meaning," Jack replied softly. "It's more than just the traditions or the gifts. It's about the people we love, the memories we create, and the hope we hold onto, even when the world is falling apart."

Emma looked around at the families gathered at the station, at the soldiers saying their goodbyes, at the small groups of people huddled together for warmth. She could feel the weight of their struggles, their fears, but also the quiet strength that bound them together. They were celebrating Christmas not because it was easy, but because it was necessary. It was a way to remind themselves that, despite everything, they still had each other.

A lump formed in her throat as she watched a young boy hand his mother a small, handmade ornament—a simple wooden star carved with clumsy hands. His mother's face lit up as she accepted it, her eyes filled with tears, and she knelt down to kiss the boy's forehead.

It was such a small moment, but it was full of love.

"Look," Jack said, nodding toward the far end of the platform.

Emma turned just in time to see the train doors close with a heavy clang. The engine roared to life, and with a sharp whistle, the train began to pull away from the station. The soldiers inside waved through the windows, some with brave smiles, others with somber expressions. Their families waved back, tears glistening in their eyes as the train disappeared into the snowy night.

A QUIET SETTLED over the station once the train was gone. Emma could feel the sadness in the air, the pain of separation, but also something else—a quiet resilience, a determination to keep going, even when the future was uncertain.

Jack looked down at her, his gaze steady. "You see, Emma, love doesn't fade when times are hard. It grows stronger. These people may be saying goodbye, but they aren't giving up. They're holding on to hope, to each other. And that's the true spirit of Christmas."

EMMA SWALLOWED HARD, trying to process everything she had seen. This wasn't the kind of Christmas she had expected, but in a way, it was more powerful than any holiday she had ever experienced. It was raw, real, and full of emotion. It made her realize that love, in its truest form, wasn't about the perfect moments or the grand gestures. It was about the small, quiet acts of kindness and the strength to keep going when the world around you was falling apart.

As the snow continued to fall, Emma felt a shift inside her. The pain of her breakup, the disillusionment she had carried with her for so long, felt a little lighter now. Maybe, just maybe, there was still hope for her, too.

JACK GAVE HER A SMALL SMILE. "Ready to go back?"

Emma nodded, though part of her wasn't quite ready to leave this moment behind. She took one last look at the station, at the families who were holding each other close, and then, with a deep breath, she took Jack's hand.

In an instant, the world blurred again, the sound of the train whistle fading into the distance as the snowy town disappeared from view.

They were gone, but the memory of that Christmas would stay with her forever.

Breaking Traditions – Disco Christmas (1970s)

The moment Emma blinked, the world around her exploded into vibrant color and sound. Gone was the quiet, snow-blanketed suburban street of the 1950s, replaced by a riot of flashing lights, bold patterns, and the unmistakable pulse of disco music reverberating through the air. They stood in the middle of a crowded city square, surrounded by an electric energy that was unmistakably 1970s. It felt like a celebration of life itself, with Christmas at its core, but in a way she had never experienced before.

NEON SIGNS BLINKED OVERHEAD, reflecting off the shiny storefront windows that were lined with tinsel, bold holiday displays, and posters advertising the latest disco hits. The once-familiar sounds of classic Christmas carols were remixed with a funky bassline, and Emma's heart raced as she took it all in—the bold, carefree atmosphere that felt worlds away from the warm, quiet nostalgia of the 1950s.

"Well," Emma said, turning to Jack with a raised eyebrow, "this is... different."

Jack grinned, his eyes gleaming with amusement. "Welcome to the 1970s. A decade where everything was bold, free, and full of self-expression. Christmas was no exception."

Emma couldn't help but laugh. The entire scene was a kaleidoscope of wild fashion and vibrant decorations. People walked by in flared pants, sequined tops, and high-heeled boots, their hair styled in wild curls or sleek, voluminous waves. A group of teenagers in platform shoes danced in the middle of the street, their moves loose and uninhibited, as if the very air itself demanded freedom and fun. It was as if the entire city had turned into one massive holiday party.

CHRISTMAS TREES LINED THE SQUARE, but they were nothing like the carefully trimmed, traditional trees Emma was used to. These were decked out in metallic garlands, oversized ornaments, and twinkling multicolored lights. The scene was louder, more chaotic, and far from the cozy family gatherings of the past—but there was something about it that made Emma's heart beat faster. It felt alive.

Emma glanced over at a makeshift stage in the center of the square, where a band was setting up, dressed in glittering jumpsuits that sparkled under the lights. People were already gathering around, their movements loose and unselfconscious, ready to dance to whatever beat the night offered.

"CHRISTMAS WITH A LITTLE MORE GROOVE, HUH?" Emma said, smiling at the infectious energy all around her.

"Exactly," Jack replied, his voice carrying a hint of nostalgia. "The 1970s were all about breaking free from expectations—

letting go of the old ways and embracing new possibilities. It was a decade that challenged traditions, and that applied to everything—including love."

Emma tilted her head, intrigued. "What do you mean?"

Jack gestured toward the crowd. "Look around. The 70s were a time when people began questioning the status quo—when love started to take on new forms, and relationships were no longer bound by convention. It was a time of liberation, in more ways than one."

As they continued walking through the square, Emma noticed a couple sitting at a small outdoor café, laughing and chatting over hot mugs of something that steamed in the cold night air. They looked unconventional in every way—the woman had short, spiky hair dyed electric blue, and the man wore a flowing shirt with vibrant patterns that clashed with his bright red bell-bottoms. Despite their striking appearances, it was the way they looked at each other that caught Emma's attention—completely absorbed in one another, as if the world around them didn't exist.

DRAWN TO THEM, Emma approached the couple, feeling the pull of curiosity she couldn't quite explain. Jack followed close behind, watching quietly.

"Hi," Emma said, stepping closer. "Mind if I join you for a moment?"

The woman looked up with a wide smile, her eyes twinkling in the streetlights. "Of course! The more, the merrier! Christmas is all about connection, isn't it?"

Emma smiled and slid into the chair across from them. "It certainly seems that way here. You both look like you're having a great time."

"We always do," the man said, grinning as he put his arm

around the woman. "Especially this time of year. We love the holidays—but we like to do them our own way."

Emma leaned in, intrigued. "What do you mean?"

The woman chuckled, her blue hair catching the light as she shook her head. "We don't really do the whole traditional thing. No turkey dinners or big family gatherings for us. We threw out the rulebook a long time ago. Every year, we create our own traditions—ones that feel right for us."

Her words struck Emma. The idea of creating their own traditions, free from the weight of societal expectations, felt like a revelation. She had always clung to the idea of what Christmas *should* be—what everyone expected it to be. But here was a couple who had let all that go, embracing the freedom to celebrate the way that made them happiest.

The man chimed in, his voice easy and warm. "We spend Christmas Eve dancing at the disco, and Christmas morning we sleep in. Later, we'll head to our friends' place for a potluck—it's all about sharing what you love with the people you care about. No pressure, no expectations."

Emma leaned back in her chair, the weight of their words sinking in. She had spent so many years trying to live up to everyone else's idea of what Christmas—and love—should look like. The big family gatherings, the perfect dinners, the picture-perfect relationship. But what if it didn't have to be that way? What if she could let go of those expectations and carve out something new—something that felt authentic to her?

"It sounds freeing," Emma said softly. "To let go of tradition like that."

. . .

The woman nodded, her expression softening. "It is. Once you stop trying to live up to what everyone else thinks you should be, you find yourself a lot happier. That's the thing about love, too—it doesn't have to look a certain way. It just has to feel right. And once you embrace that, the rest falls into place."

Emma's heart twisted at the truth of those words. For so long, she had been holding on to a version of love that didn't fit—trying to force herself into a mold that had only left her feeling empty. The breakup, the loneliness she had felt afterward—it all stemmed from that same pressure to conform to an ideal that wasn't hers. But now, sitting here in this loud, vibrant square surrounded by people who had broken free of those expectations, she felt something shift inside her.

Jack, who had been watching the exchange in silence, finally spoke. "Love, like Christmas, doesn't have to follow the rules. It can be anything you want it to be. This time is all about defying expectations and finding your own path. The 70s were good at teaching that lesson."

Emma smiled at him, realizing how much this journey was changing her. Each era had shown her something new—something about love, about life, about herself. And now, here in the rebellious, carefree atmosphere of the 1970s, she felt the final piece of that puzzle fall into place.

The disco music thumped louder in the background, and she watched as more people gathered around the stage, their movements wild and joyous. There were no stiff, traditional rules here—just the freedom to be who they were, to love how they wanted, and to celebrate in whatever way felt right for them.

Emma looked back at the couple, feeling a rush of gratitude. "Thank you," she said softly. "I didn't realize how much I needed to hear that."

. . .

THE WOMAN WINKED. "Anytime. Just remember—there's no right or wrong way to celebrate, or to love. There's only your way."

As Emma and Jack stood to leave, the music swelled, and she couldn't help but feel a tug to join the growing crowd of dancers. Jack, sensing her hesitation, raised an eyebrow. "Care for one last dance before we go?"

Emma laughed, feeling lighter than she had in a long time. "Why not? When in the 70s, right?"

They joined the crowd, the rhythm of the music guiding their movements as the lights pulsed around them. For the first time in years, Emma let go—of the past, of her fears, of the pressure to be anything but herself. She danced, laughed, and allowed herself to be swept up in the freedom of the moment.

And as the night wore on, she realized that maybe, just maybe, Christmas—and love—could be whatever she wanted it to be.

THE WORLD SPUN AGAIN, but this time, the sensation wasn't quite as jarring. Emma closed her eyes, bracing herself for wherever—or whenever—Jack would take her next. She felt the air around her shift, growing warmer, and when she opened her eyes, she was no longer standing on a snowy train platform during wartime. Instead, the crisp air had a pleasant, fragrant quality—like pine and freshly baked cookies—and soft music filled the background, as though the world had just turned on a record player.

EMMA BLINKED, taking in her surroundings. They were standing on a wide, quiet street lined with neat, identical houses, each one decked out with twinkling lights, wreaths on the doors, and large red bows tied around mailboxes. The neighborhood looked like something out of a dream, every detail perfect and picturesque, as if someone had taken a scene straight out of a Norman Rockwell painting and brought it to life.

In the distance, she could hear the laughter of children and the low rumble of car engines idling as families loaded shopping bags into the trunks of shiny cars. It felt like a snapshot of another era—an era she had only ever glimpsed in black-and-white movies or old Christmas cards.

"The 1950s," Jack said beside her, his voice soft, yet with a touch of amusement as he watched Emma take it all in. "This was a time when Christmas really came into its own—suburban life, department store windows, the birth of holiday specials on TV. It was a decade that loved its traditions."

Emma's breath caught in her throat as she took in the scene before her. Unlike the heavy, somber atmosphere of the 1940s, this felt lighter—almost too perfect. A feeling of nostalgia washed over her, though it wasn't even her own nostalgia. This wasn't her time, yet something about it stirred something deep inside her.

She turned slowly, her gaze sweeping across the street, where she saw families gathered inside warm, glowing houses. In one window, a family decorated a tall Christmas tree, the children hanging tinsel with eager hands while their parents looked on, smiling. In another house, a group of people sat around a large dinner table, passing dishes of food as the adults laughed and the kids squabbled over a gingerbread house. It was the kind of Christmas she had only seen in old movies—wholesome, uncomplicated, and full of the simple joys that seemed so far away from her own life.

As they walked down the street, Jack stayed close, letting her take it all in. "This was a time when families were the heart of Christmas," he said, nodding toward one of the houses. "There was a sense of togetherness that people clung to, even in the most ordinary moments."

EMMA STOPPED in front of a large department store, its windows dressed in extravagant holiday displays. She gazed at the mannequins dressed as Santa Claus, elves, and shoppers bundled in coats with packages piled high in their arms. It was all so familiar, yet so far from what she knew. Inside, the store was bustling with activity—shoppers darting between the counters, sales clerks wrapping gifts in shiny paper, and children pressing their noses to the glass in awe of the latest toy displays.

She could hear the sound of Christmas carols drifting through the air, and for a moment, she was transported into the holiday she'd always imagined as a child—the perfect Christmas, where everyone was happy, and everything was as it should be.

"They didn't have much, did they?" Emma asked, her voice quieter now. "At least, not like we do today. No fancy gadgets or extravagant presents. Just... this."

JACK SMILED SOFTLY, his gaze following hers. "No, they didn't have much in the way of material things. But they had something else—something that's easy to lose sight of."

"What's that?"

"Simplicity," Jack replied. "They cherished what they had. Family, home, and the little things that made life rich. It was a different kind of Christmas. One less focused on what they could buy, and more on who they could share it with."

Emma nodded, her chest tightening with a mix of longing and realization. She'd spent so many Christmases wrapped up in the hustle, the expectations, the pressure to create a perfect holiday—chasing after the idea of something she could never quite grasp. Here, in this simpler time, it was all laid out in front of her. Families, togetherness, laughter. The warmth of home.

As they continued walking, Emma noticed a small family across the street, gathered outside their house to string lights on the porch. A father balanced precariously on a ladder, while his wife stood below, offering instructions with a wide smile on her face. Two children, a boy and a girl, ran in circles around them, chasing each other and giggling as they tried to catch snowflakes on their tongues.

The sight tugged at something deep inside her, something she hadn't allowed herself to feel in a long time. It wasn't just the image of a happy family—it was the sense of belonging, of being part of something greater than herself. She had grown so distant from her own family over the years, especially after the breakup. She had withdrawn, convinced that she didn't need anyone. But now, watching this simple, joyful scene, she wondered if maybe she'd been wrong.

"They're happy," Emma said softly, her eyes lingering on the family.

"They are," Jack agreed. "But not because everything is perfect. It's the imperfections that make it real. They're happy because they're together, and that's what matters to them."

Emma swallowed hard, her mind racing. She thought of her own family, of the holiday traditions she'd slowly let slip away. The big Christmas dinners, the decorating of the tree, the silly holiday movies they used to watch together. Somewhere along the way, she'd stopped caring about those things. She'd become so focused on her own hurt, her own loneliness, that she'd distanced herself from the people who had always been there for her.

Jack seemed to read her thoughts. "Christmas isn't about perfection, Emma. It's about the connections we make, the love we share, and the memories we create, even when things aren't ideal."

Emma nodded, her throat tightening as the weight of his words sank in. She had spent so long pushing people away, trying to protect herself from more hurt, but in doing so, she had lost sight of what really mattered. Her family, her friends—they were the ones who had always been there, offering love and support, even when she didn't want to accept it.

SUDDENLY, she heard the familiar strains of a song coming from one of the nearby houses. A piano played the opening notes of "Have Yourself a Merry Little Christmas," and Emma couldn't help but smile as the voices inside joined in, harmonizing perfectly. It was like something out of a classic holiday movie—a scene she had watched a hundred times, but now, standing here, it felt different. It felt real.

They passed another house, where a group of neighbors had gathered around a crackling firepit, mugs of hot cocoa in hand as they sang carols and laughed together. The warmth of their camaraderie reached Emma, even from a distance, and she found herself smiling, something deep inside her softening.

"This," Emma whispered, her voice barely audible. "This is what I've been missing."

JACK DIDN'T SAY ANYTHING, but she felt his presence beside her, steady and patient. He had shown her this moment for a reason—

not just to look back at the past, but to remind her of what she still had, what she could still reclaim.

"Family, home, love," she murmured, almost to herself. "I've been pushing them away. But maybe... maybe I don't have to anymore."

Jack turned to her then, his expression warm but knowing. "You don't. The past may hold beautiful memories, but it's the present that gives you the chance to create new ones."

Emma exhaled slowly, her heart lighter than it had been in a long time. She realized now that the perfect Christmas didn't exist—not in the way she had imagined, anyway. The perfect Christmas was the one where you let go of the need for everything to be flawless and embraced the love and connection that had always been there.

The world around them began to shimmer again, and Emma knew their time in the 1950s was coming to an end. But as the scene faded, she felt something different this time—a sense of peace, of understanding.

When the world righted itself again, and the familiar streets of modern-day New York City reappeared, Emma turned to Jack, her heart full.

"I'm ready," she said softly. "To go home. To my family."

Jack smiled, nodding. "That's the spirit of Christmas, Emma. Home, love, and the people who matter most."

And for the first time in a long time, Emma knew that was exactly where she belonged.

Unveiling the Past – Jack's Secret (1920s)

The world shifted once again, but this time, the air felt different—warmer, sweeter, as if it carried the scent of champagne and possibility. When the haze cleared, Emma found herself standing on a grand street, illuminated by golden light spilling from towering buildings. The sound of distant jazz filled the air, the sultry notes of a saxophone mixing with the hum of laughter and conversation from well-dressed partygoers.

IT WAS THE 1920S, *and it was spectacular.*

ALL AROUND HER, the energy buzzed with decadence and freedom. Women in shimmering flapper dresses, their lips painted dark and their hair in sleek bobs, danced to the rhythm of the music that seemed to pour from every corner. Men in sharp suits and fedoras mingled, their voices rising with cheer as they tipped their glasses and wished each other a merry Christmas. It was a different kind of holiday celebration—wild and carefree, fueled by jazz, champagne, and the glamour of the Roaring Twenties.

EMMA TURNED TO JACK, who was standing beside her, his usual calm demeanor carrying a new weight, a heaviness she hadn't noticed before. He seemed to blend into this era as if he belonged here, his posture more relaxed, his gaze lingering on the sights with a kind of bittersweet familiarity. His suit, more formal than anything she had seen him wear before, fitted him perfectly, as though this time period had been waiting for him to return.

"This... this is incredible," Emma said, her voice filled with awe as she took in the lavish surroundings. "The 1920s."

Jack gave a soft smile, but there was something in his eyes—something distant. "It was a time like no other. There was an energy, a spirit of rebellion and freedom after the war. People were hungry for life, for joy, and Christmas was no exception."

They walked down the bustling street, passing a line of glittering holiday storefronts where elaborate displays of luxury goods and ornaments sparkled in the windows. Every detail was a reflection of the opulence and extravagance of the era, and Emma could feel the excitement in the air—the sense that the world was alive with endless possibility.

BUT AS THEY CONTINUED, Emma noticed something else about Jack. He wasn't just showing her the 1920s—he was *returning* to it. The way he moved, the way he looked at the people and places around him, it wasn't with the same detached curiosity he had shown in the other eras. There was a familiarity here, a deep connection, and for the first time, Emma sensed there was more to Jack's story than he had let on.

As they walked, they arrived at a grand hotel, its exterior

adorned with glittering lights and garlands. The heavy oak doors were flanked by doormen in sharp uniforms, welcoming guests who stepped out of gleaming cars, their laughter and chatter filling the cold night air.

Jack paused, his gaze lingering on the entrance. "This is where we're going tonight."

EMMA LOOKED AT HIM, her curiosity growing. "What is this place?"

Jack's smile was faint, tinged with a sadness she hadn't seen before. "The Starlight Hotel. One of the grandest venues in the city during the Roaring Twenties. And the site of one of the most famous Christmas Eve parties New York ever saw."

Emma felt a flicker of something—unease, perhaps, or anticipation—as they approached the entrance. The doorman tipped his hat as they walked inside, and immediately, the world around them burst into vibrant life. The grand ballroom was a spectacle of shimmering gold, with chandeliers hanging from the ceiling like glittering constellations. Guests in their finest attire swirled around the room, dancing to the upbeat tempo of a live jazz band that played from a raised platform. Laughter, music, and the clink of glasses filled the space, creating a perfect picture of festive revelry.

Emma's breath caught in her throat. "This is like something out of a dream."

JACK STOOD BESIDE HER, his expression unreadable as he watched the festivities. "It was," he said softly, almost to himself. "It was perfect."

There was a weight in his words that made Emma turn to him, her eyes searching his face. "You were here, weren't you?"

Jack's gaze remained on the dancers, but his eyes darkened, filled with a sadness that reached across the decades. "Yes," he whispered. "This was my Christmas."

Emma felt a jolt of surprise. She had assumed Jack was merely guiding her through history, showing her different moments in time. She hadn't realized that this—this era, this night—was personal to him.

"Tell me," Emma said gently, stepping closer. "Tell me what happened."

JACK LET OUT A SLOW BREATH, his shoulders sagging ever so slightly as if the weight of his past had finally caught up with him. "I was a different man then, Emma. A younger man. I lived in this city, in this world. The 1920s were wild, full of excitement and promise. I was... in love."

The words hung in the air, and Emma felt the sting of them. There was pain in his voice, the kind that only comes from a loss that time could never quite heal.

"Her name was Clara," Jack continued, his voice quieter now. "She was everything to me. We met here, at this very party, one Christmas Eve. She was dazzling—full of life, full of joy. We were inseparable after that night. Every Christmas, we'd come here together, dancing until dawn, laughing, making plans for the future."

He paused, his jaw tightening. "But one Christmas Eve, it all changed. Clara fell ill—suddenly, without warning. There was nothing the doctors could do. She passed away on Christmas Eve, the night of this party. The same night we were supposed to meet under that chandelier, just like we always did."

. . .

Emma's heart sank as she listened, feeling the depth of Jack's grief. She could picture it—the two of them, full of love and hope, and then the sudden, brutal loss that had shattered everything. It made sense now, the way Jack carried himself with an air of timelessness, the way he seemed to understand love and loss in a way few others did.

"I couldn't stay in this world anymore," Jack said, his voice thick with emotion. "I couldn't bear the thought of living through another Christmas without her. That's when I was given the watch—the one you hold now. The man who gave it to me said it could take me to any Christmas, past or future, and that I would become its keeper."

Emma's eyes widened in understanding. "So you've been... traveling through time ever since? Looking for something?"

Jack nodded, his gaze distant. "At first, I was searching for her. I thought maybe if I could find the right moment, the right Christmas, I could bring her back, or at least relive those memories. But over time, I realized it wasn't about finding Clara. It was about healing. About accepting that time moves forward, even when you don't want it to."

Emma's heart ached for him. She had seen Jack as a guide, someone who understood the magic of time, but now she realized he was more like her than she had thought—someone who had been hurt by love, who had lost the person who meant the most to him. His journey wasn't just about nostalgia; it was about healing, about trying to make sense of the past and find peace in the present.

"You've been searching for closure," Emma said softly, her voice trembling slightly.

Jack nodded, finally turning to look at her, his eyes filled with the weight of decades of heartache. "I've been searching for a way to let go."

Emma felt an unexpected connection between them, something deep and unspoken. She had been running from her own pain, distancing herself from the people she loved because she didn't want to face the loss and disappointment that had come with her broken heart. But now, standing here with Jack, she realized that healing didn't come from avoiding the past. It came from facing it, accepting it, and finding a way to move forward.

"Jack," Emma said quietly, stepping closer, "maybe this is the Christmas where you stop running."

Jack's gaze softened, his eyes locked on hers as the noise of the party faded into the background. "Maybe it is."

And for the first time, Emma saw him not as the keeper of time, but as a man—someone who had loved and lost, just like her. And maybe, just maybe, this journey wasn't just about rediscovering Christmas. It was about finding love and hope again—together.

As the jazz band played on and the lights sparkled above them, something shifted between Emma and Jack, something that felt like the beginning of a new story. A story of healing, of letting go of the past, and of finding something new in the present.

Christmas, after all, was a time for miracles.

The air was sharp and electric as Emma blinked and found herself once again in the heart of New York City—but this wasn't the New York she knew. The neon lights, brighter than ever before, cast a rainbow of colors onto the bustling streets. Above her, massive billboards displayed ads for everything from the latest high-tech gadgets to flashy fashion trends. The familiar hum of the city was dialed up to eleven, a mix of honking cabs, blaring music, and the constant buzz of holiday shoppers weaving through the throngs of people.

Emma took a deep breath, trying to get her bearings. The 1980s had arrived in full force.

Gone were the quaint, carefree vibes of the 1970s. Now, the city seemed almost larger than life, pulsing with an energy that was both thrilling and overwhelming. The sidewalks were jammed with people—businessmen in oversized suits rushing to meetings, teenagers with brightly colored hair and Walkmans blasting in their ears, and shoppers juggling bags and boxes as they darted in and out of stores that screamed *SALE!* in bold, blocky lettering. Christmas was everywhere, but it was louder, brighter, and more commercial than anything Emma had ever seen.

She glanced over at Jack, who stood beside her with his hands in his coat pockets, taking in the scene with an easy smile. "Welcome to New York in the 1980s," he said, his voice barely audible over the noise. "Big, bold, and unapologetic."

Emma let out a breathy laugh, shaking her head. "It's like everything's been turned up to max volume. Is this how Christmas was back then?"

Jack nodded, his eyes scanning the flashing department store windows. "The 80s were all about consumerism—more is more. The city was booming, and Christmas became part of the show. The bigger the display, the better."

Emma's gaze followed his, landing on a storefront that looked more like a stage set for a Broadway show. The windows were filled with animatronic Santas, elves, and glittering reindeer, all moving in perfect synchronization to a loop of "Jingle Bell Rock" that blared from speakers outside the building. Crowds gathered to watch, their faces lit by the glow of the neon lights and flashing signs overhead.

"It's... a lot," Emma admitted, though she couldn't deny there was something captivating about it all.

THEY MOVED with the flow of the crowd, Emma marveling at how every block seemed to outdo the last in terms of holiday spectacle. Every store was decked out in Christmas decor, from shimmering tinsel and gigantic bows to towering Christmas trees covered in gleaming ornaments. There was no mistaking the fact that this was the height of the holiday shopping season, and everyone seemed caught up in the frenzy.

Jack led Emma toward the corner of Fifth Avenue and 49th Street, and when they turned the corner, the sight of Rockefeller Center took her breath away. The iconic ice rink stretched out before them, packed with skaters, their laughter echoing through the crisp evening air. Above them, the towering Rockefeller Christmas tree stood in all its glory, draped in thousands of twinkling lights that shimmered against the night sky. It was grand, over-the-top, and unmistakably beautiful.

"This is..." Emma paused, searching for the right word. "Incredible. But also... chaotic."

JACK SMILED KNOWINGLY. "It's easy to get lost in all of it, isn't it? The lights, the shopping, the rush. In the 1980s, the holidays became more about what you could buy, what you could show. But if you look closely, you'll still find the real heart of it."

Emma raised an eyebrow, intrigued by his words. "What do you mean?"

Jack gestured to the ice rink, where a couple was skating hand in hand, their faces flushed with joy despite the cold. Nearby, a family huddled together, sipping hot chocolate as they laughed and watched the skaters glide by. The commercialization was everywhere, yes, but so were these small, authentic moments of love and connection that still managed to shine through the chaos.

Emma stood there for a moment, watching the scene unfold. Couples, families, and friends filled the ice rink and the surrounding plaza, and despite the neon signs flashing around them, there was something undeniably human about the way they interacted. They were there for the simple pleasure of being together, sharing laughter and warmth in the midst of the city's hustle.

"Even with all this... noise," Emma said softly, "you can still see it. The love. The moments that actually matter."

Jack nodded, his eyes softening. "Exactly. The 80s may have been flashy, but at its core, Christmas didn't lose its meaning. It's easy to get distracted by the glitter and the glitz, but those small, quiet moments are what last."

They walked further into the plaza, and Emma noticed a group of friends gathered near the massive tree, laughing and exchanging gifts wrapped in bright, shiny paper. One of them—clearly the ringleader—handed out presents with exaggerated flair, causing the others to burst into laughter. They hugged, snapped Polaroid photos, and clinked their plastic cups of hot cider in a makeshift holiday toast.

Nearby, a woman knelt down to tie her daughter's ice skates, her face filled with affection as the little girl eagerly tugged at her hand, wanting to rush onto the ice. A couple sat on a nearby bench, their hands entwined, content to watch the world go by as they shared a quiet moment amid the bustling crowd.

Emma's heart softened as she watched these snippets of life unfold. It wasn't about the grand displays or the extravagant gifts. It was about these small, real connections—the kind that made everything else fade into the background.

"I think I'm starting to get it," Emma said after a long silence. "Every era we've been to... it's shown me something different about love, about Christmas. Here, it's like the distractions are louder than ever, but that just makes the real moments even more precious."

Jack glanced at her, a faint smile tugging at the corners of his mouth. "That's the thing about Christmas, Emma. No matter how the world changes, no matter how big or busy or commercial it gets, the core of it remains the same. It's about love. It's about finding those moments, even when everything around you is chaos."

Emma nodded, feeling a sense of peace wash over her. She had been so caught up in her own life, her own struggles, that she had forgotten how to look for those moments. She had let the distractions take over—her breakup, her disillusionment with love, her distance from her family. But here, in the heart of this vibrant, chaotic city, she realized that love still found a way to shine through, even in the busiest of places.

As they stood there, a light snow began to fall, the flakes catching in the glow of the lights from Rockefeller Center. Emma tilted her head back, watching the snow swirl down, feeling a quiet joy settle in her chest. She didn't need the perfect Christmas, the perfect love. She just needed to look for the moments that mattered—because those moments were always there, if she let herself see them.

Jack's voice broke through her thoughts, soft and steady. "Ready to head back?"

Emma took one last look at the scene before her—the laughter, the lights, the warmth that radiated from the people around her—and nodded. "Yeah. I think I'm ready."

As they began to walk away, leaving the bright lights of 1980s New York City behind, Emma felt lighter, more sure of herself. She had been searching for something this whole time, and now she realized it had been with her all along—the understanding that love and connection, no matter how small or quiet, were what truly made Christmas special.

And maybe, just maybe, she was ready to embrace that in her own life too.

Falling in Love Through Time

The days blurred together in a kaleidoscope of eras as Emma and Jack continued their travels through time. Each Christmas they visited revealed a new layer of history, a different celebration of the holiday, and more glimpses into the heart of what truly mattered. But with each step they took, with every new Christmas they explored, something else began to change—something between them.

At first, Emma had dismissed it as simple companionship. After all, Jack had been her guide through this surreal journey, the one constant presence amid the whirlwind of time. But slowly, something deeper had emerged. She found herself drawn to his wisdom, his charm, and especially his vulnerability. The more he opened up to her, the more she realized that his heart—burdened by the weight of his past—was much like hers.

. . .

And Jack, despite the centuries he had lived, was not as immune to love as he pretended to be.

They found themselves in an 18th-century ballroom one snowy evening, surrounded by elegant revelers in powdered wigs and silk gowns, the air thick with the scent of mulled wine and candle wax. A string quartet played a gentle waltz, the notes mingling with the flickering glow of candlelight. Emma had traded her modern coat and boots for a gown of deep crimson, its heavy fabric making her feel both out of place and strangely timeless.

She had always admired the beauty of these historical moments, but tonight her focus wasn't on the room's opulence or the traditions of the past. It was on Jack.

He stood across from her, his tall frame regal in a black coat with polished buttons, his eyes watching her with an intensity she had grown accustomed to but still hadn't fully understood. As the waltz continued, the dancers twirled around them in slow, graceful circles, but Emma and Jack stayed rooted in place, the space between them humming with unspoken words.

Emma broke the silence first, her voice soft but steady. "You never told me how you ended up with the watch. Not the whole story."

Jack hesitated, his gaze flickering toward the dancers for a moment before returning to her. "It was given to me, as I said. After Clara... after I lost her, I met someone who understood the burden I carried. He told me that the watch could offer me a different kind of life, a life where time wasn't linear. But there was a cost."

. . .

"A cost?" Emma asked, her heart beginning to pound, sensing the gravity of his words.

Jack nodded, his expression darkening. "Time isn't meant to be manipulated, Emma. The watch lets me travel through Christmases past, present, and future, but it keeps me apart from the flow of time itself. I've never been able to stay in one place for long—never able to fully live in any moment." He paused, his voice quieting. "Until you."

The words hit Emma like a jolt, and she stared at him, her breath catching. The air between them crackled with emotion, and suddenly, the distance that had always existed between them felt unbearable.

"Jack..." she whispered, unsure of what to say, but knowing that something had changed. The connection they shared had deepened in ways she hadn't anticipated, and now, standing here with him, she realized that she didn't want this journey to end.

Jack took a step closer, his eyes never leaving hers. "I wasn't expecting this," he said, his voice low and rough. "I've traveled through time for so long, carrying the weight of the past. I thought I could help you find what you were missing, but somewhere along the way, I found something I didn't know I was missing, too."

Emma's heart raced, her mind spinning. She had been so disillusioned with love before—so convinced that it wasn't meant for her. And yet here she was, standing before a man who had lived through centuries of heartbreak and loss, and finding herself drawn to him in ways she hadn't expected. But it wasn't just attraction. It was something more—something profound and real.

"What happens now?" she asked, her voice trembling with the weight of the question.

. . .

Jack's face darkened slightly, and he looked down at the pocket watch in his hand. The gold casing glinted in the candlelight, but Emma noticed something different—tiny cracks running along its surface, faint but growing. Her stomach twisted.

"I don't know how much time we have left," Jack admitted, his voice heavy. "The watch is malfunctioning. It's been damaged by all the years of use. I've felt it slipping, losing control over where it takes us, how long we can stay."

Emma's pulse quickened, fear knotting in her chest. "What do you mean?"

Jack met her gaze, his expression full of regret. "The watch won't last much longer. Our time—our time together—could run out at any moment."

Emma's heart sank. She had grown to care for Jack in a way that terrified her, and the idea of losing him now, after everything they had been through, felt unbearable. She hadn't even realized how deeply her feelings had grown until the prospect of losing him became real.

"Is there any way to fix it?" Emma asked, desperate for a solution.

Jack shook his head, his eyes filled with sorrow. "Time can't be fixed, Emma. It's fleeting. Even for me."

The truth of his words settled over her like a heavy blanket, and Emma felt the weight of her own heartache rising to the surface. She had spent so long avoiding love, avoiding the vulnerability that came with it, but now, standing in the middle of this timeless ballroom, she realized that love wasn't something you could escape. It found you, even when you weren't ready for it.

. . .

Jack stepped closer, his hand reaching out to take hers. His touch was warm, grounding her in the moment despite the chaos swirling in her mind. "Emma, I never meant for this to happen. I didn't expect to feel... this. But I can't deny it anymore. I care about you. Deeply."

Emma's heart pounded in her chest. "I care about you too, Jack. More than I thought I could."

For a moment, the world around them seemed to still. The music, the dancers, the flickering candlelight—it all faded into the background, leaving just the two of them in the quiet space between past and present.

"But what happens when the watch stops working?" Emma asked, her voice trembling with fear. "What happens to us?"

Jack's expression softened, his thumb brushing gently over her hand. "I don't know. But I do know that time isn't something we can control. All we have is the moment we're in. And right now, I'm here with you."

Emma swallowed hard, the lump in her throat threatening to choke her. She wanted to believe that this moment could last forever, that somehow they could defy time and stay together. But Jack was right—time was fragile, fleeting, and impossible to hold onto.

"I'm scared, Jack," she whispered, her voice barely audible.

"So am I," Jack admitted, his eyes filled with the same vulnerability she felt inside. "But I'd rather have this moment with you than none at all."

In that instant, Emma made her choice. She didn't know how much time they had left, but she wasn't going to waste it on fear.

She had spent too long running from love, and now that it was right in front of her, she wasn't going to let it slip away.

Without another word, Emma closed the distance between them and kissed him. The world seemed to pause around them as their lips met, the chaos of time and history falling away. It was just the two of them, together in that fleeting, fragile moment. The kiss was gentle at first, tentative, but it quickly deepened, the weight of everything they had been through pouring into the connection.

W͟h͟e͟n͟ ͟t͟h͟e͟y͟ ͟f͟i͟n͟a͟l͟l͟y͟ ͟p͟u͟l͟l͟e͟d͟ ͟a͟p͟a͟r͟t͟, both breathless, Emma felt a sense of clarity wash over her. She didn't know what the future held, but for the first time in a long time, she wasn't afraid of it.

"Whatever happens," she whispered, her forehead resting against Jack's, "we'll face it together."

Jack smiled, his eyes softening with affection. "Together."

And for now, that was enough.

The Final Choice – Christmas Eve

The air was still, unnervingly quiet as if time itself had paused to wait for what was coming. Emma and Jack stood together on a snowy street corner, the glow of twinkling lights reflecting off the frost-covered ground. The snow fell in soft, slow flurries, but for once, Emma couldn't appreciate the beauty of it. Her heart pounded, and her hands trembled as she held the pocket watch, now more fragile than ever, its surface marred by fine cracks that shimmered like spiderwebs.

THE MAGIC WAS SLIPPING AWAY. *She could feel it, like sand running through her fingers.*

JACK STOOD BESIDE HER, his expression grave yet calm, as if he had accepted what was coming long before she had. His usual air of mystery had been replaced by something more vulnerable, a quiet resignation that made Emma's heart ache even more.

"How long do we have?" Emma asked, her voice barely above a whisper, afraid of the answer.

Jack glanced at the watch, his eyes filled with a sadness that cut through her. "Not long."

They had traveled through so many Christmases together—shared moments in eras long gone, each one teaching Emma something new about love, family, and the magic of the holiday. But now, the journey was ending. The watch, once a powerful talisman of time, was breaking down, and with it, the thread that bound them together across these different centuries.

Emma looked up at Jack, her heart heavy with the decision she knew she had to make. She had come to care for him in ways she never expected, and the idea of leaving him, of returning to her own time without him, felt unbearable. But deep down, she knew she couldn't stay here, lost in the past, no matter how much she wanted to.

"You could come with me," Emma blurted out suddenly, her voice filled with desperation. "Come back to my time. We could figure it out. We could—"

Jack smiled softly, his eyes full of affection but also sorrow. "I wish I could, Emma. But I don't belong in your time. My place is here, where I came from. You have your life, your family, your future. You can't stay in the past with me, no matter how much we want to pretend time doesn't matter."

Tears welled in Emma's eyes, her chest tightening as she fought against the reality of his words. She had come so far with Jack—learned so much from him. He had shown her a new way of seeing the world, of understanding love and its many forms, but now, at the end of their journey, she was faced with an impossible choice.

"I don't want to lose you," Emma whispered, her voice trembling as tears spilled down her cheeks.

Jack reached out, gently brushing a tear away with his thumb. His touch was warm, tender, and it made her want to cling to him, to hold on to this moment for as long as she could.

"You're not losing me," he said softly. "I'll always be with you. Time may separate us, but love... love is timeless, Emma. It's the one thing that transcends all of this."

EMMA SHOOK HER HEAD, her heart breaking as she realized that this was it—the moment she had been dreading since the watch first began to show signs of its fading magic. "How can you say that? We've shared so much, and now it's all slipping away."

Jack's smile was sad but resolute. "Because I've learned something from you, too. Love isn't about holding on to the past or wishing for things we can't have. It's about being present, about embracing the moments we have, even if they're fleeting. And our time together—it's been more than I ever expected."

The weight of his words pressed down on her, making it harder to breathe, harder to accept what was coming. Emma glanced down at the pocket watch in her hand, the cracks growing more pronounced, the faint ticking slowing as if it were winding down to its final moments.

SHE HAD TO CHOOSE. Stay here, frozen in time with Jack, or return to her life in the present, where she belonged. Both options felt devastating, and yet, one was the only path forward.

Jack stepped closer, his face inches from hers. "You belong in your world, Emma. It's where you're meant to be. You have so much waiting for you—a future, new love, a chance to build something real. Don't lose that because of me."

Emma's vision blurred with tears, and her voice cracked as she spoke. "I don't want to leave you."

He leaned in, pressing his forehead against hers, his breath warm against her skin. "You're not leaving me. Our time together has changed me, just as it's changed you. That will never disappear. But you have to go back. You have to live."

EMMA CLOSED HER EYES, trying to gather the strength to say goodbye. Every part of her wanted to stay—to hold on to Jack and this connection they had built across time. But deep down, she knew Jack was right. This wasn't her world. She had a life waiting for her, and even though the idea of returning to it without him felt unbearable, she couldn't let the past keep her from moving forward.

With a trembling breath, Emma opened her eyes and looked up at Jack, her heart aching. "I'll never forget you."

Jack smiled, though his own eyes glistened with unshed tears. "I'll never forget you either, Emma."

She hesitated for a moment, then leaned in and kissed him—softly at first, then with all the emotion she had been holding back. It was a kiss filled with love, longing, and the painful knowledge that this would be the last time they would be together.

WHEN THEY PULLED APART, Emma felt the world around them begin to shift, the edges of reality blurring as the magic of the pocket watch reached its breaking point.

"Goodbye, Jack," Emma whispered, her voice barely audible over the wind that had begun to swirl around them.

Jack nodded, his gaze steady, filled with love. "Goodbye, Emma. Be brave."

And then, as the world dissolved into a flurry of snow, Jack disappeared, his figure fading into the swirling white. The pocket watch in Emma's hand gave one final, soft tick before it shattered, the magic within it gone.

THE SNOW CONTINUED to fall around her, and as the world of the past melted away, Emma found herself standing alone in the middle of modern-day New York City. The familiar hum of the present surrounded her—car horns, people chatting on their phones, Christmas lights twinkling in the windows of shops.

Emma wiped the tears from her cheeks, her heart heavy with loss but also filled with something new. She had fallen in love through time—experienced moments that would stay with her forever—and though her heart ached for Jack, she knew he had been right.

Love transcended time. And even though their paths had diverged, she would carry him with her, always.

As she turned to face the city, the snow still falling gently around her, Emma took a deep breath, feeling the pulse of the present draw her forward. She had returned to her world, her time, and though the future was uncertain, she was ready to face it—with love.

A Timeless Christmas Love

The streets of New York City shimmered with the magic of Christmas. The soft glow of holiday lights reflected off the wet pavement, casting a golden hue across the bustling sidewalks. The festive energy was palpable—couples huddled close, families laughed as they carried bags of last-minute gifts, and children, their faces bright with joy, pointed at the elaborately decorated shop windows. Everywhere Emma looked, she saw Christmas in its purest form—love, laughter, and the sense of wonder that had once seemed so distant to her.

But now, walking hand-in-hand with Jack through those very streets, everything felt different. Everything felt possible.

Jack's fingers intertwined with hers, warm and steady, and with every step they took together, Emma felt her heart swell. This was the life she had thought she might never have—a life filled with love, with the promise of shared moments and new Christmas memories that stretched far beyond the bounds of time.

"I still can't believe this is real," Emma said softly, glancing up at Jack as they walked past the brightly lit Rockefeller Center, where skaters twirled on the ice below the towering Christmas tree.

Jack smiled down at her, his eyes filled with warmth. "Believe it, Emma. It's as real as anything we've experienced—maybe even more real."

Emma smiled, leaning into him as they continued their walk through the heart of the city. The night was crisp, the air cold enough to turn their breath into soft clouds, but neither of them noticed the chill. They were too lost in the moment, too wrapped up in each other and the magic that surrounded them.

"Do you ever think about the past?" Emma asked after a long silence, her voice contemplative. "All the places we've been… the people we met…"

Jack nodded, his expression thoughtful. "I do. Every time I visited another Christmas, I thought it was the past that held all the answers. But now I know it's the present that matters most. What we do with the time we have, right here and now—that's what counts."

Emma looked up at him, her heart swelling with love. "I'm glad you're here. I'm glad we found each other."

Jack squeezed her hand gently. "I'm glad, too. I didn't think it was possible to love again, after all the time I spent running from the past. But you showed me that love doesn't fade, no matter how much time passes. It just takes on new forms, in new moments."

They continued walking through the city, the festive lights and decorations casting a warm, golden glow around them. The sound of carolers filled the air, their voices rising in perfect harmony as they sang "Silent Night," and Emma felt a familiar warmth bloom in her chest—the same warmth she had felt as a child, when Christmas still held all its magic.

But this time, the magic was even more powerful. This time, she wasn't just looking at the lights or listening to the music; she was living in the very heart of the season, with Jack by her side.

The city was alive with Christmas cheer, and as they strolled past windows filled with bright, twinkling lights, Emma realized something important: it wasn't just the lights, the music, or the decorations that made Christmas special. It was the people you shared it with. It was the love that filled those moments, the connections that transcended everything else.

As they walked, they passed a small group of children huddled around a window, their eyes wide with wonder as they gazed at a festive holiday display. Inside, mechanical elves danced around a brightly decorated Christmas tree, while a cheerful Santa waved from his sleigh. The children's laughter filled the air, and Emma couldn't help but smile at the pure joy on their faces.

Jack watched the scene with a soft expression, then turned to Emma. "You've changed me, you know."

Emma raised an eyebrow, surprised. "I changed you?"

Jack nodded, his voice tender. "Before I met you, I thought love was something I could only find in the past. Something that had already slipped away, like Clara. But you showed me that love doesn't have to be bound by time. It can exist in the present, in moments like this."

Emma's heart ached with emotion, and she leaned into Jack, resting her head against his shoulder. "You've changed me, too. I thought love was something that had passed me by, that it wasn't meant for me anymore. But you... you showed me that it's never too late to open your heart again."

Jack smiled, pressing a soft kiss to her forehead. "Then I guess we both learned something from each other."

THEY CONTINUED TO WALK, their steps slow and unhurried, as the city around them buzzed with holiday energy. Snow began to fall in soft, delicate flakes, dusting the streets and the tops of the brightly decorated trees. Emma watched as the snow fell, feeling the quiet peace that came with the season settle over her.

Finally, they reached the edge of Central Park, where a quiet, snow-covered pathway led deeper into the park, away from the hustle and bustle of the city. The lights grew softer here, the sounds of the city fading into the background, replaced by the quiet stillness of the falling snow.

JACK STOPPED, turning to face her. "Emma, I know we don't know what the future holds, but I do know one thing. I want to spend it with you. Wherever it takes us."

Emma looked up at him, her heart full of love, and smiled. "I want that, too."

They stood there for a moment, just the two of them, surrounded by the twinkling lights of the city, the snow falling softly around them. In that moment, Emma knew that everything she had experienced—every Christmas they had visited, every lesson she had learned about love and family—had led her to this. To him.

And in Jack's eyes, she saw the promise of a future filled with new Christmas memories. A future where love, like Christmas itself, would continue to transcend time and endure forever.

· · ·

With the snow gently falling around them, Jack leaned in and kissed her, a kiss filled with the magic of the season, the hope of new beginnings, and the timeless love they had found together.

And as they stood there, wrapped in each other's arms, Emma knew that no matter what the future held, this—this love—was the greatest Christmas gift she had ever received.

Because love, like Christmas, was truly timeless.

Sunlight streamed through the curtains of Emma's apartment, warming the room with the soft, golden glow of Christmas morning. She blinked awake, the familiar sounds of the city below slowly filtering into her consciousness—the honking of distant car horns, the faint hum of people going about their day.

For a moment, everything felt strangely ordinary. But as her eyes adjusted to the light, the memories of the past days came rushing back, and with them, the ache of what she had lost.

Jack.

Emma sat up slowly, her heart heavy, but not entirely broken. The journey she had taken through time—visiting Christmases from different eras, each with its own lesson about love, family, and the things that mattered most—had changed her in ways she hadn't expected. She was no longer the woman who had been disillusioned with Christmas, tired of love, and hesitant to let herself be vulnerable. She had seen love in all its forms, from the quiet resilience of wartime Christmases to the rebellious, carefree spirit of the 1970s. And through it all, Jack had been her guide, her anchor.

But he was gone now. He had remained in the past, where he belonged, while she had returned to the present to face her life and her future. And though her heart ached for him, she knew he had been right. Life had to move forward. She had to move forward.

She slid out of bed and wrapped herself in a soft robe, padding over to the window. Snow was falling lightly outside, the world covered in a pristine white blanket that seemed to muffle the usual chaos of the city. Christmas lights twinkled from the buildings across the street, and despite everything, Emma felt a strange sense of peace.

As she stood there, watching the snow drift lazily to the ground, she thought about the people she loved—her family, her friends, the people she had distanced herself from for so long. Maybe it was time to reconnect, to reach out and rebuild those relationships. She had learned so much from the Christmases she had visited: that love wasn't perfect, but it was worth fighting for; that family, no matter how imperfect, was a gift to cherish; and that the present, not the past, was where life happened.

With a deep breath, Emma turned away from the window and walked toward her small Christmas tree, the soft glow of the lights casting a warm, comforting light across the room. She smiled to herself, feeling a sense of renewal—a new beginning, just as Jack had promised. She was ready to face her life again, with hope and a heart more open than it had been in years.

. . .

But just as she was about to head into the kitchen to make herself a cup of coffee, there was a knock at the door.

Emma froze, her heart leaping into her throat. For a moment, she stood still, unsure if she had imagined it. Who could be knocking on Christmas morning? Her family was across town, and none of her friends had mentioned coming by. The knock came again, this time a little louder, more insistent.

With her heart pounding in her chest, Emma slowly walked to the door, her mind racing. She pulled it open—and there, standing in the falling snow, was Jack.

He looked exactly as she remembered, dressed in the same coat he had worn during their travels through time, his dark hair dusted with snowflakes. But there was something different about him now—something more grounded, more real. His eyes, those deep, warm eyes she had come to know so well, were filled with the same affection, the same vulnerability she had seen before. But this time, there was no sadness, no lingering pain of the past. There was only hope.

"Jack?" Emma's voice was barely a whisper, her breath catching in her throat.

Jack smiled, his face lighting up with the same quiet, knowing smile that had always made her feel safe. "Merry Christmas, Emma."

Emma blinked, hardly daring to believe what she was seeing. "How... how are you here?"

Jack stepped forward, his eyes never leaving hers. "The watch may have broken, but the magic—our magic—was stronger than time. I couldn't stay in the past, not after everything we shared. Somehow, I found a way back to the present. To you."

Emma's heart swelled with emotion, her eyes filling with tears. "But I thought... I thought we'd never see each other again. You said time couldn't be changed."

Jack nodded, his expression softening. "I thought that too. But I've come to realize that love—real love—can transcend time. It's not bound by the rules we think govern the world. Christmas is a time for miracles, and I think this is ours."

Tears spilled down Emma's cheeks as she stepped forward, closing the distance between them. She reached out, placing her hand against Jack's cheek, feeling the warmth of his skin, the reality of him standing here in front of her. "I don't understand how this is possible," she whispered, her voice trembling. "But I don't care. You're here."

Jack gently brushed a tear from her cheek, his touch as tender as it had been when they had kissed for the first time. "I'm here. And this time, I'm staying."

Emma let out a soft, broken laugh, the weight of her emotions overwhelming her. She threw her arms around him, pulling him into a tight embrace. Jack's arms wrapped around her, holding her close, and for the first time in what felt like forever, Emma felt truly at peace.

They stood there for a long moment, wrapped in each other's arms, the snow continuing to fall around them. The world outside seemed to fade, leaving only the two of them in their own quiet bubble of warmth and love.

When they finally pulled apart, Jack looked down at her, his eyes filled with quiet determination. "I don't know what the future holds, Emma. But I know that I want to face it with you. If you'll have me."

Emma smiled, her heart lighter than it had been in years. "I want that too, Jack. I don't care what comes next, as long as we're together."

Jack's smile deepened, and he leaned in, pressing a soft, lingering kiss to her lips. It was a kiss full of promise, of hope, of the future they were about to build together.

When they finally broke apart, Emma felt as though a weight had lifted from her shoulders. The fear, the uncertainty, the heartache—it was all gone. In its place was a quiet, steady love that she knew would carry them both forward.

"Come inside," Emma said softly, taking Jack's hand. "Let's start Christmas together."

Jack nodded, stepping through the door as Emma closed it behind them. They stood together in the warm glow of her apartment, the lights of the Christmas tree twinkling in the background, and for the first time in a long time, Emma felt like she was exactly where she was meant to be.

This was her new beginning—a Christmas miracle she had never expected, but one she was ready to embrace with all her heart. And as she and Jack stood together, hand in hand, she knew that no matter what challenges the future might hold, they would face them together.

Because sometimes, love really was timeless.

Afterword by Evangeline Winters

Dear Readers,

As I write this afterword, I find myself reflecting on the journey we've just taken together through time, love, and the magic of Christmas. *A Timeless Christmas Love* is a story that's been close to my heart for a long time. It started as a seed of an idea—what if love could truly transcend time? What if the spirit of Christmas, which connects us to traditions, family, and nostalgia, could also bring us closer to our own hearts and to one another, no matter where we are or how broken we may feel?

This story is about more than just time travel or romance. It's about the discovery that love, in all its forms, can heal us, guide us, and offer us hope, even when we think we've lost it. Emma's journey through the Christmases of different decades mirrors the emotional path many of us take in our own lives. We hold onto memories, we carry wounds from the past, and we sometimes let the chaos of life blind us to the beauty in front of us. But as Emma learns, it's never too late to open your heart, to find love again—whether it's with someone new or in the relationships you already have.

At its core, *A Timeless Christmas Love* carries the message that love, like Christmas, is not confined by the passage of time. Love can bloom in the simplest of moments, in the shared laughter of family, the touch of someone dear, or even in the quiet spaces of reflection. No matter what challenges or heartaches we face, love is the constant thread that ties us to our past, our present, and our future.

Through Emma's story, I hope you've been reminded of the power of hope, the importance of family, and the beauty of living in the present while cherishing the past. And I hope Jack's story reminds us all that even when we feel bound by the past, there is always a path forward—one that leads to healing and new beginnings.

As you close this book and return to your own holiday traditions, I invite you to hold onto the magic of this season. Remember that no matter how much time passes, the love we share—whether with family, friends, or that special someone—is what makes this time of year so extraordinary.

Thank you for joining me on this journey through time, love, and Christmas. May your holidays be filled with joy, and may you always carry with you the timeless gift of love.

Warmly, **Evangeline Winters**

Message of the Story:

The message of *A Timeless Christmas Love* is that love, in all its forms, transcends time and space. It reminds us that love is not confined to the past or future—it is something we can carry with us, no matter what era or situation we find ourselves in. Christmas, with its traditions, warmth, and connection, is a time when we are invited to reflect on what truly matters: the people we love and the moments we share.

The story encourages us to embrace vulnerability, to let go of past hurts, and to open ourselves to the possibilities of love and connection in the present. It's a reminder that time may change, but the power of love endures—just like the spirit of Christmas, which is timeless.

www.ingramcontent.com/pod-product-compliance
Lightning Source LLC
LaVergne TN
LVHW050029080526
838202LV00070B/6981